MW00949267

Christmas Eve

The Joy of Giving

Positive Spin Press
Rhode Island, U.S.A.

For Genevieve
and her great granddaughters
Amelia, Josie, Ellie and Gena

.ISBN: 0-9773096-2-2

Special Thanks to JaGaJo & Brandi Gifford

Published by Positive Spin Press
www.positivespinpress.com

Distributed by Independent Publishers Group
www.ipgbook.com 1-800-888-4741

Printed in China

Once upon
a winter's day
before the snow
came out to play
A fairy who makes little toys
came to learn of
Christmas Joys...

Sweet Eve got a letter by special dispatch
Sent by Magic Express to her home in the patch

She wasn't surprised to get mail from an elf
But this special note was from SANTA HIMSELF!

"Dear Eve, How we need you," poor Santa had jotted
"The elves all have elfpox! They're all polka-dotted!

We're so busy giving the elves proper care
That we can't, for my big Christmas journey, prepare!

The whole world would be grateful, and most of all, me
If you'd come to the North Pole immediately!"

So, Eve grabbed her wand and she flew with great speed
All the way to the north to help Santa in need

She met dear old Santa and Nana and shivered,
"Here I am – oo..oo..one frozen fairy delivered!"

"Put these on!" said Nana, "then come in and rest
For, at the North Pole, even trees must get dressed!"

NORTH POLE

"Oh, Santa!" said Eve, "it would be my delight
to help you prepare for your Christmas Eve flight"

"But what can I do?" she then shrugged with dismay
"what child wants a small toy on Chris-ti-mas Day?"

Understanding her fear, Santa scratched his great chin,
"Let me tell you how this Christmas story begins...

For, it's not about size or the grandness of gift
But of spirit and how we can help it to lift!"

“The very first Christmas brought life’s great example
Of the love just one person can bring – and it’s ample!

For in a small stable, a baby was born
God’s gift to a world that was broken and torn

Away from the crowds, he was born in the heart
of a family of love – a most wonderous start!

Because of the wisdom and love He would bring
He would come to be known as Lord Jesus, Our King"

"His greatness was humble, he needed no showing
of fine, fancy duds or large crowds who were crowing

He came here and said that God loves us – each one!
and to lift up our hearts to what we can become

Most - he taught love – for life, neighbor and self
These lessons inspire us – me and these elves"

"So remember, that very first Christmas did give
One small Gift to be shared by each person who lives!

But that Gift grew each day filling up many hearts
For 'most two thousand years – over all the world's parts!"

And with that, Santa turned to bring elves more popsicles
As Nana Claus tapped on Eve's wing, where it tickles

INFIRMARY
TICKLE

"When Santa was young, well before we were wed
A Christmas elf gave him a shiny new sled

He loved it so much! He loved pulling and riding
He'd even do chores if it kept his sled gliding

He carried home wood for the winter night's fire
Or sacks for his neighbors whose arms were too tired

With each act of kindness, that sled's magic grew
And with work and with love it became something new!

Little things grow, and with love you will see
They flourish and change most miraculously!"

“Perhaps you have heard of two brothers named Wright
Who, inspired by toys, brought the whole world to flight!

Young Orville loved dinosaurs – making them roar
And Wilbur loved trains, and laid tracks on the floor”

ULLAM
BUBS

"One Christmas when Orville was just about six
His new pterodactyl did loopdy-loop tricks

And Wilbur's new passenger car really had
Some tiny play people who looked just like Dad

First each had his fun, then they started to share
When both of them found a surprise waiting there!

'We can make people fly!' they imagined and schemed
and before long, those boys had done just what they dreamed!"

"So you see, now, the elves have made quite a fine art
Of knowing just how to plant seeds in the heart

And Santa brings toys, for you know what they say
To learn, grow and share is most fun done through play!

But the true gift, my dear, is the heart's inspiration
When *that* is received, it's a real celebration!"

THE JOY
OF GIVING

As Nana Claus spoke, something caught their attention
The reindeer outside looked as if in detention

"Poor deer," whispered Nana, "they've been working for weeks
They're exhausted and bored, with no life in their cheeks!"

"I've got it!" said Eve as she called out their names
"I can make them some toys! They can play reindeer games!"

"Well, that brightened things up! Ho Ho Ho!" Santa said
And Eve was so happy and proud she turned red!

"Look at them now! What you've done! How they're living!
And look at your smile! You feel The Joy of Giving!

For, there's no gift that can make a heart more elated

Than seeing the gift you gave ap-pre-ci-a-ted!"

By Christmas Eve night, Eve was ready to go
And the elves were recovering nicely, and so...

"Let's go!" Santa called, "Let us be God's reminder
That people should play more, and laugh, and be kinder!"

Santa's eyes beamed, like the berries on holly
"It's The Joy of Giving that keeps this elf jolly!"

And Eve wasn't concerned that her toys were too small
She knew that her love made the best gifts of all

So, now, what can you give? Love for what you receive!
There is no greater gift you can give Christmas Eve!

POOF!
TALLULA
QUINN